The Little Red Hen

A little red hen once
found some grains of wheat.
She showed them to her friends—
the cat, the pig, and the duck.

1

"Who will help me plant this wheat?" said the little red hen.

"Not I," said the cat.
"Not I," said the pig.
"Not I," said the duck.

"Then I will plant it myself,"
said the little red hen.
And she did.

The wheat grew tall and golden. All the animals could see that it was ready to be cut.

"Who will help me cut this wheat?" said the little red hen.

"Not I," said the cat.
"Not I," said the pig.
"Not I," said the duck.

"Then I will cut it myself,"
said the little red hen.
And she did.

Then it was time to grind
the wheat into flour for baking.
"Who will help me grind this
wheat?" said the little red hen.

"Not I," said the cat.
"Not I," said the pig.
"Not I," said the duck.

"Then I will grind it myself,"
said the little red hen.
And she did.

When the wheat was ground into flour, the little red hen carried it back to her kitchen.

"Who will help me bake the bread?" said the little red hen.

"Not I," said the cat.
"Not I," said the pig.
"Not I," said the duck.

"Then I will bake it myself,"
said the little red hen.

And she did.

Soon she pulled the bread
out of the oven.

"Who will help me eat the
bread?" said the little red hen.

"I will," said the cat.
"I will," said the pig.
"I will," said the duck.

"No, you will not!" said the little red hen.

"I planted the wheat.

I cut the wheat.

I ground it into flour for baking.

I baked the bread.

So I will eat it all by myself."

And she did.